How we saw the world

To my grandson, Tehonikonrateh (Andrew)

Other books by C.J. Taylor:

How Two-Feather was saved from loneliness
The Ghost and Lone Warrior
Little Water and the gift of the animals
The secret of the white buffalo
Bones in the basket: Native stories of the origin of people
The monster from the swamp: Native legends of monsters, demons, and other creatures
The Messenger of Spring

Copyright © 1993 by C.J. Taylor

Published in Canada by Tundra Books, *McClelland & Stewart Young Readers*,
481 University Avenue, Toronto, Ontario M5G 2E9

Published in the United States by Tundra Books of Northern New York,
P.O. Box 1030, Plattsburgh, New York 12901

Library of Congress Catalog Number: 92-83960

Also available in a French edition, ***Et le cheval nous a été donné: Légendes amérindiennes sur la création***, ISBN 0-88776-357-X

Canadian Cataloguing in Publication Data

Taylor, C.J. (Carrie J.), 1952-
    How we saw the world : nine Native stories of the way things began

ISBN 0-88776-302-2 (bound)   ISBN 0-88776-373-1 (pbk.)

1. Indians of North America – Folklore. 2. Creation – Folklore.
3. Nature – Folklore. 4. Legends – North America. I. Title.

PS8589.A88173H69 1998   j398.2'097'0408997   C97-932770-9
PZ8.1.T39Ho 1998

We acknowledge the support of the Canada Council for the Arts for our publishing program.

Design by Michael Dias

Printed in Hong Kong by South China Printing Co. Ltd.

Sources

Bemister, Margaret, *Thirty Indian Legends of Canada*, Vancouver: Douglas & McIntyre, 1973.
Brown, Dee, *Teepee Tales of the American Indian*, New York: Holt, Rinehart & Winston, 1979.
Erdoes, Richard, and Ortiz, Alfonso, eds., *American Indian Myths and Legends*,
    New York: Pantheon Books, 1984.
Legends of Our Nations, Cornwall Island, Ontario: North American Indian Travelling College, 1984.
Mayo, Gretchen W., *North American Indian Stories: Earthmaker's Tales*,
    New York: Walker and Company, 1990.
Mayo, Gretchen W., *North American Indian Stories: More Earthmaker's Tales*,
    New York: Walker and Company, 1990.

Some of the designs used in this book are inspired by drawings found in *American Indian Design & Decoration* by LeRoy H. Appleton, published by Dover Publications Inc., New York.

3 4 5 6   01 00 99 98   2 3 4 5 6   02 01 00 99 98

How we saw the world
Nine Native stories of the way things began

C.J. Taylor

Tundra Books

The legends

Introduction

When the Europeans first arrived in our lands, they thought us pagans without spirituality. They condemned us as lost souls because they did not understand our forms of worship.

But our religion was everywhere around us. We saw the work of the Creator in everything: the sun, the moon, the wind, the ground, and in the animals and plants given us for food. We had, and still have, a daily sense of the Creator and we worship by showing love and respect for our Mother Earth.

If you wish to understand any culture, look at its folklore, tales and legends. The nine stories in this anthology are only a few of the thousands we have told through the centuries. They try to explain the mysteries of nature to us and I hope they will help you see the world as we see it.

I chose these stories to paint because I found each one illuminated our relationship to nature in an exciting, informative, and even humorous, way. I can almost hear the laughter of children as they listened to an elder explain why owls and rabbits look the way they do.

Imagined here are the origins of the beautiful: waterfalls and butterflies; of natural disasters such as tornadoes and unending winters and our human attempts to deal with them; of animals like horses who helped us live better and dogs ready to die to save their master. And there are warnings too: what happens to communities if people don't care for each other and what will happen to the world if all of us do not keep nature in balance.

I thank you for allowing me to share a small part of our history with you.

Nia wen.

C.J. Taylor

ALGONQUIN

The birth of Niagara Falls

There once lived an old man on top of a mountain so high that he could see the ocean many days away. Because he lived among the clouds everything about him was silvery white: his long hair, his house of birch bark, even his five daughters.

All five were very beautiful. Their clothes were made from the foam of rapids, their sandals from the spray of water against the rocks and their wings from feathers carried in the wind. When they flew with birds around their mountain home, their long white hair floated behind them.

One day the sisters decided to leave their father's lodge to play on the rocks by the sea. As they flew over the mountains they caught sight of a bare cliff, higher and steeper than anything they had ever seen. The youngest sister, who was always looking for new adventures, said, "Let's play on this rock." She dove off it like a bird and the other sisters followed. It was so much fun they flew back up and dove down again and again and soon they forgot about the distant sea. The sun set and the moon came out and still they played.

In the morning, the cliff was no longer bare. Great amounts of water poured over it, rushing, foaming, sparkling in the sun. The five sisters enjoyed the cliff so much they decided to play there forever.

And if you go to Niagara Falls, you can still see the sun shine on the foam of their dresses, the spray from their sandals and the feathery mist from their wings.

Why butterflies cannot sing

One sunny day in late summer the Great Creator looked down at children playing in the sunlight and felt sad that fall was coming.

Soon the trees would lose their leaves, the flowers die and it would be too cold for the children to play outside.

"I am going to make something new and beautiful while there is still color everywhere," he thought.

So the Great Creator took some gold from the sun, blue from the sky, white from the clouds and black from the shadows. He took green, yellow and red from the trees and more colors from the flowers. He put them into a bag and added the songs of birds.

He shook the bag and dropped it among the children. When they opened it, butterflies of every color came flying out, playing with the children and singing the loveliest songs.

The children were very happy and thanked the Great Creator.

But a songbird flew up to the Creator and said, "When you made us, you gave each bird its own song. But now you have given our songs to these new creatures."

The Great Creator agreed. "I should not have done that," he said. "They are so beautiful, they will give joy to all who look at them. They don't need to sing."

And the Great Creator took away the song from the butterflies and left them only their colors.

How Eagle Man created the islands of the Pacific Coast

Once long ago all the people in a village became very selfish. They did not help their neighbors. They did not share food. They did not even take very good care of their children.

One day the father and mother of a boy left to go hunting and never returned. The boy did not know whether they had been killed or had just gone off and forgotten him. Desperate and alone, he went to his nearest relative, an uncle, for help.

The uncle didn't want to have anything to do with the orphaned boy. "I have no time to care for this boy," he announced. "Does anyone want to adopt him? If not, let the whole village look after him. I'm not going to do it."

The villagers refused to help. "If you won't look after him, why should we? Don't bother us with your problems."
The uncle, who was not only selfish but cruel as well, decided to get rid of his nephew. He took the boy down to the beach and put him in a canoe. "Sleep here tonight," he ordered. "You'll be comfortable. It's cooler than inside."

When the boy fell asleep, the uncle cut the canoe adrift and watched it float off toward the ocean. "That's the last I'll see of him," he thought, pleased with himself.

The water carried the canoe far along the shore and finally up onto a beach near the village of the Eagle people. They were kind and they welcomed the boy as if he were sent as a gift. Everyone cared for him and he grew up to be a fine young man. The chief's daughter fell in love with him, and when they were married the chief gave him the name of

Eagle Man, a cloak of feathers and a very special present: he was taught how to fly.

Eagle Man was happy with his new family, but he could not completely forget the people in the village who had refused to care for him and the uncle who had tried to get rid of him. As he grew older, the memory came back to haunt him day and night. "I must go back there," he told his wife. "I must."

Eagle Man put on his feather cloak and flew to the village where he was born. As he passed over it, he caught sight of his uncle and was overcome with anger. He swooped down, caught the cruel man by the hair and lifted him off the ground.

A villager saw this and tried to hold the uncle back by grabbing at his feet. He too was lifted up. Soon the entire village was hanging onto each other and being carried off.

Eagle Man flew over the ocean and began dropping the villagers one by one into the water. "You did not love and care for each other when you were together," he told them. "Now you will be separated from each other forever."

As the villagers fell into the water, each became an island. That is why on the Northwest Coast, there are thousands of islands, all separated by water.

MICMAC

How Snowmaker was taught a lesson

One winter long ago Snowmaker came down from the North and would not leave. Spring did not come. The birds did not return. Animals hid to escape the bitterly cold winds. Snow covered the ground and ice covered the rivers, making it hard to get food. When the people went to gather firewood Snowmaker stung their ears and noses with the cold. The people feared there would be no spring, summer and autumn and that they would not be able to hunt or fish or find berries.

It was June that year before Snowmaker decided to return to his northern home and the snow started to melt. Gray Wolf called the people together. "We must teach Snowmaker a lesson. He has grown too powerful." He carved a bowl from a large log, put the last of the melting snow into it and placed the bowl in the rays of the sun. As it melted he cried out: "Snowmaker, I am not afraid of you!"

At that moment, as if to warn him, a cold wind blew in from the North. The people were frightened. "Do not anger Snowmaker," they told Gray Wolf, "or next winter will be longer and colder still."

But Gray Wolf was determined to find a way to help his people. He knew that Snowmaker was angry now and would come after him in the autumn. He worked hard all summer. He built a shelter away from the village and piled firewood around it until the shelter was hidden. He kept the furs of the animals he hunted and preserved the meat for food. And he did something different: instead of eating the animal fat as his people normally did, he melted it into oil and kept it in his wooden bowl.

13

The days grew shorter and autumn came. Cool days were followed by colder nights. One day the sun didn't come out at all. Gray Wolf knew Snowmaker was about to attack. He went into his shelter, pulled his fur robes tightly around him, built a fire and waited for Snowmaker.

Snowmaker came upon the village in a fury. For days he blew his icy breath everywhere and covered the ground with snow as he searched for his enemy. Gray Wolf huddled in his shelter and felt weak from the cold. The wind came through the cracks and made it difficult for him to keep his fire alive. "I have never been this cold," he thought.

Snowmaker found Gray Wolf's shelter and entered it with a blast of cold air. The fire flickered as if about to go out. Snowmaker laughed. "You think you can defeat me?" he sneered.

With the last of his strength Gray Wolf reached for his wooden bowl and threw the oil onto the embers. The flames leaped up and danced around wildly, lighting the shelter. Snowmaker fell back, sweating, panting. "Your fire is too hot for me," Snowmaker cried, cowering in a corner. "You have defeated me," he hissed. "But I will return." With that, he ran from the lodge, leaving a trail of melted snow in his wake. Gray Wolf felt his strength and the warmth outside return.

The people could not believe that Gray Wolf had defeated Snowmaker, not until spring arrived on time that year. Then the hunters learned from Grey Wolf to keep the oils from the animals they brought home so as to make their winter fires burn brightly.

Snowmaker still returns every year with his cold wind, ice and snow. But because of Gray Wolf, Snowmaker is no longer as powerful as he used to be.

BLACKFOOT

How horses came into the world

Long ago there lived an orphan boy whose name was Stone Cloud. He saw that his Blackfoot people did not have enough to eat and that hunters often returned to the village empty-handed. "If only I could help my people," Stone Cloud thought.

He set out on a search that took him far from his village. He crossed mountains and streams but found nothing. Finally, he came to a lake. On the other side a large herd of buffalo grazed. It could provide his people with food and clothing and tents if only he could cross the water. He sat down at the water's edge and cried.

The Water Spirit lived in the lake and heard the boy's crying. He told his son, "Go see what grieves that boy." Spirit Son swam to the surface and listened to Stone Cloud's story.

"I think my father can help you," Spirit Son said. "I will take you to him. Hold your breath and hang on to me."

Then he added a warning: "My father will offer you a gift. You will be allowed to take anything that is of the water. But be careful. Accept only the oldest mallard duck and its little ones."

Stone Cloud held on to Spirit Son's shoulders as they dove beneath the surface of the lake. He wondered why he should want a duck when there were larger animals and fish in the water. Stone Cloud was pulled deeper and deeper to the bottom of the lake.

"Why were you crying?" Water Spirit asked Stone Cloud.

16

"My people are hungry and I want to help them," the boy said. "I have been away from home searching for food and I have not found anything."

"Perhaps I can help you," Water Spirit said. "You may take anything you wish from this lake. What will it be?"

Stone Cloud remembered Spirit Son's advice and said, "The old mallard and its ducklings."

Water Spirit asked Stone Cloud many times if he was sure he wanted the ducks and each time the boy said yes.

"Very well," Water Spirit said at last. "You may take the ducks. But I warn you: when you leave the lake, you are not to look back at them, no matter how curious you are. Only when the sun rises tomorrow may you look back."

Spirit Son caught the old duck and placed a rope of braided grass around its neck. He took the old duck to the surface followed by the ducklings and gave Stone Cloud the rope. "Remember what my father said," he warned.

As Stone Cloud started the long walk back toward his village he heard the flapping of feathers behind him. During the night, the sound slowly changed to the pounding of heavy feet and the grass rope in his hand felt like leather. Stone Cloud wanted to see what had happened, but he remembered the warning and continued forward.

At last the sun rose and when Stone Cloud turned around he saw a big strange animal he had never seen before. It was followed by smaller ones. He was frightened until a voice said: "This animal will help your people so they will never be hungry again. Climb on its back and return to your village."

Stone Cloud did as he was told and rode the horse proudly into his village with the smaller horses following. It was now the villagers' turn to be frightened. "Do not be afraid," Stone Cloud told them. "These animals will hunt with us and pull heavy loads."

The Blackfoot people saw the usefulness of this new animal. It was better for carrying things than the dogs they had been using. They could ride these "elk-dogs" to where the buffalo were and hunt more easily. Horses could even carry people across water. "They are from the water," Stone Cloud said. "This is why they are at ease in it."

When Stone Cloud grew older he was made chief of the Blackfoot people. His favorite place to sit and rest was at a tree near the water because from there he could see the horses grazing in the distance.

ONEIDA

Why the dog is our best friend

There once lived a famous hunter named Wolf Runner. He went everywhere with his two wolf-like dogs. With their help he always brought back food for his village. The dogs could hear and smell game long before he saw it.

One day, Wolf Runner and his dogs spent all day hunting but found nothing. They climbed a mountain far from the village and saw no wildlife — not a bird nor an animal anywhere. A strange silence had settled over the forest.

Suddenly a terrible sound came from the trees. The dogs stopped and growled. Their fur stood up on their backs in fear. Wolf Runner had never seen them so angry — or frightened. One of the dogs looked at Wolf Runner and said, "Run back to the village as fast as you can. It is the Flying Head of the Forest. It destroys everything in its path. Run with us."

Wolf Runner could not believe he had heard the dog speak. He did not move. The dog spoke again: "You have been kind to us. You are our friend. I have been given the gift of speech to warn you. You must run. The Flying Head is coming fast."

The sound turned into a terrible scream. Wolf Runner ran back down the mountain, toward his village, his dogs keeping pace on each side. The screaming grew louder and was followed by a crackling worse than thunder. Wolf Runner looked back and saw the most terrifying sight of his life. A huge, ugly head with big yellow eyes was after him. Its open mouth contained rows of sharp fangs that ate everything in its path. The head jumped from tree to tree on wings of fire, destroying everything.

Wolf Runner ran faster. The dog looked up at him and spoke again, "Get to the village. I will try and hold it back. Go on without me."

Behind him, as he ran, Wolf Runner heard the dog barking and then a wild yelp of pain. He realized his friend had given his life to save him.

Again Wolf Runner felt the hot breath of the Flying Head on his back. The other dog said, "It is my turn. I will fight the monster. You keep running to the village."

Wolf Runner could see his village by now and he ran faster. Behind him, he heard barking, then another yelp of pain, and knew his other friend had died to save him. He ran across the clearing, almost out of breath, and reached the edge of the village, safe at last.

The people huddled outside their longhouses, watching the Flying Head across the clearing. Showers of sparks flew from its mouth and flames shot out of its awful eyes. Behind it the trees had all been burned to stumps already. But with no trees to carry it, the ugly head could not reach the village. Slowly, the head disappeared, leaving behind only smoke.

Wolf Runner thought of his friends with sadness. "I know we will be together in the Land of Spirits," he said. "Until then dogs should be treated as our best friends. Anyone who is cruel to them will never reach the Land of the Spirits."

The first tornado

One summer day long ago the hot sun beat down on the people as never before. The heat came down like a blanket, leaving them with no air to breathe. The animals had all disappeared. Plants were dying in the dry earth. Even the snakes did not come out of their holes. The people felt they would soon dry up and die like the grass around them.

"Help us, please," they begged the Medicine Man. "Or we will become nothing but dried up bones.

"Go to the riverbed," the Medicine Man ordered, "and find some moist, red clay. Go immediately and bring it to me before it dries up."

The Medicine Man took the clay and, while the people watched, he shaped it into a horse with large white wings. He blew into its nostrils until the first sign of life appeared. Then he asked everyone to help him.

As they all blew together, the horse grew larger and larger. Its wings started to move and pull it upwards. Soon the people could hold it down no longer. The horse flew up and around in a circle overhead, faster and faster. The wind from its wings blew everywhere, lifting tipis off the ground, breaking branches from the trees and swirling dust so that no one could see.

"What have you done?" the people cried out to the Medicine Man. "This wind is worse than the heat!"

The Medicine Man called to them over the noise of the wind storm. "It will be all right soon." Then he shouted: "Horse! Go to your new home behind those dark clouds."

As the people watched, the horse disappeared behind the clouds, the skies calmed and the longed-for rains came, cooling them, filling the river again and returning life to the plants.

Now whenever terrible heat is followed by a tornado, the people know the horse has come down again. But they also know when it goes back behind the clouds, there will be rain to cool and refresh them.

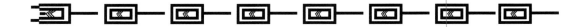

MOHAWK

Why rabbits and owls look the way they do

One day the Great Creator was making animals, carefully one at a time. Each animal told him how it wanted to look and the Great Creator tried to fulfill every wish.

When it was Rabbit's turn, he said: "I want the longest ears and the longest legs in the world."

The Great Creator began forming Rabbit. He made long, soft ears and long strong back legs. Just as he was working on the front legs, he was interrupted by Owl, who was waiting next in line to be made.

"I'll tell you how I want to look," Owl said.

The Great Creator stopped him: "Be quiet! Wait your turn."

But Owl went right on talking. "I want the best of everything. I want every other bird to be jealous of me. I want the most colorful feathers, the longest, most graceful neck, the most beautiful eyes and a song that will make the other birds wish they could sing like me."

The Great Creator was furious. "I told you to wait your turn!" he thundered. "I do not like anyone watching me work. Do you think it is easy trying to make every animal and bird different, giving each what it wants? Go away. I will call you when I am ready."

"Whoo, whoo, whoo," hooted Owl. "I'll watch if I want to."

"You will NOT!" shouted the Great Creator. He was so angry he dropped Rabbit, grabbed Owl and went to work.

"You want colorful feathers? Yours will be gray and brown."
And he rubbed Owl in the mud. "You want a graceful neck?
You will not have a neck." And he pushed Owl's head into his
body. "You want beautiful eyes? You will have big eyes that
only see in the night. You want to sing the nicest songs? You
will hoot the rest of your days." And so, the Great Creator
made Owl one of the strangest looking birds in the world.

Meanwhile Rabbit was so scared by the Great Creator's
anger that he ran off to hide. His back legs were longer than
his front ones and he had to hop everywhere. He also never
got over his fright and remained a nervous animal.

But at least he got his long, soft ears and was able to move
very fast, even without long front legs.

How the world will end

The earth is held up by a tall, tall tree trunk.

This tree trunk is like a sacred dance pole. The spirits of all living creatures swirl around it in a beautiful rhythmic dance. Great Beaver is slowly gnawing at the pole. When he is displeased, he gnaws faster and the pole gets weaker.

We displease Great Beaver when we interfere with the rhythm of the dance. Great Beaver knows and gnaws faster and the pole tips a little. If Great Beaver gnaws through the pole, the earth will fall.

That is why all creatures, especially people, must keep the earth in balance.

So as not to anger Great Beaver.

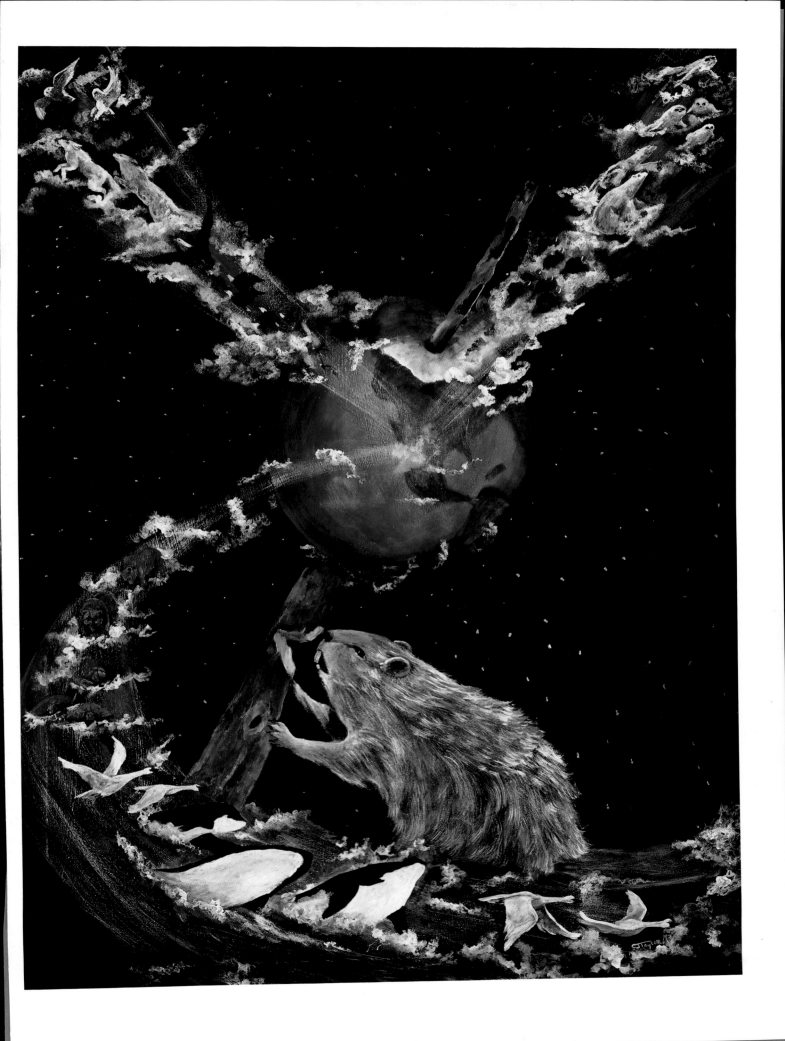